W9-DAD-307

The Magic School Bus

BUTTERFLY AND THE BOG BEAST

A BOOK ABOUT INSECT CAMOUFLAGE

SCHOLASTIC INC.

New York Toronto London Auckland Sydney
Mexico City New Delhi Hong Kong Buenos Aires

From an episode of the animated TV series
produced by Scholastic Entertainment Inc.
Based on *The Magic School Bus* books
written by Joanna Cole and illustrated by Bruce Degen.

TV tie-in book adaptation by Nancy E. Krulik and illustrated by the Thompson Brothers.
TV script written by Brian Meehl, George Bloom, and Jocelyn Stevenson.

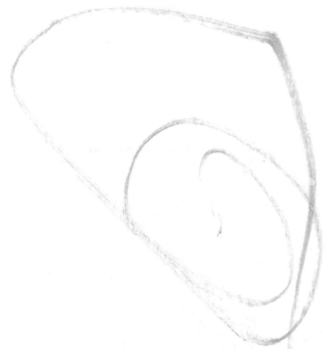

ISBN 0-590-50834-2

31 30 29 28 27 26 25   8 9/0

Printed in the U.S.A.

Being in Ms. Frizzle's class is always surprising. She has a way of turning everything into an exciting adventure — even picking a name for our class soccer team!

We had exactly six hours before the biggest soccer game of the year, and we still didn't have a name — or a mascot — for our team.

"We need a mascot that's different!" said Keesha.

"It has to be so surprising the other team won't know what hit them!" added Carlos.

Hey, isn't that Arnold's cousin, Janet, over there?

Quick, let's find someplace to hide!

Phoebe glanced at the book in her hand. It was all about butterflies and moths. "I got it!" she shouted with delight.

We were all excited. "What? WHAT?" we asked her.

Phoebe spread her arms out like wings. "The Walker Elementary BUTTERFLIES!"

Suddenly we weren't so excited.

"You want to name our soccer team the Butterflies?" Ralphie asked. He sounded disgusted.

"And have a mascot that's small..." added Wanda.

"And swattable..." continued Tim.

"And beautiful?" Keesha finished in disbelief. "We want to be a tough, talented team, not a *pretty* team."

Just then, Arnold's know-it-all cousin, Janet, climbed down from the bleachers to join us.

I am your favorite cousin, right, Arnold?

You're my ONLY cousin, Janet.

Janet put her hands on her hips.

"You want a mascot that's totally different?" asked Janet. "Then get this. How about . . . the Walker Elementary Bog Beasts!"

"It's so surprising they won't know what hit them," said Keesha.

Wow! Everyone thought that was a great idea! Everyone except Arnold, that is.

"What's a Bog Beast?" he asked.

Suddenly *we* were surprised by Ms. Frizzle. Flapping wings, she glided down from the ceiling. And she was dressed in a butterfly costume!

"A crafty question, Arnold," she said. "Anyone know what a Bog Beast looks like? Janet?"

Janet's face turned beet red. "Well, it's, ah, probably, ah..."

Dorothy Ann pulled out her notebook. "According to my research, a bog is wet, soggy ground, like a swamp."

That was when Ms. Frizzle got that time-for-a-field-trip look in her eyes. "Seems to me, then," she said, "a swamp's the place to find a Bog Beast! To the swamp!"

Does the swamp have butterflies, too?

The swamp has all sorts of surprises.

I just knew she'd say that. *Sigh.*

We all climbed aboard the Magic School Bus and fastened our seat belts. We weren't surprised when the bus turned off the main highway and onto a small dirt road. We weren't surprised when it drove into a misty forest, either. We weren't even surprised when the bus went right into a swamp, gurgled, gargled, and . . . turned into a swamp boat. When you're in Ms. Frizzle's class, you get used to things like that.

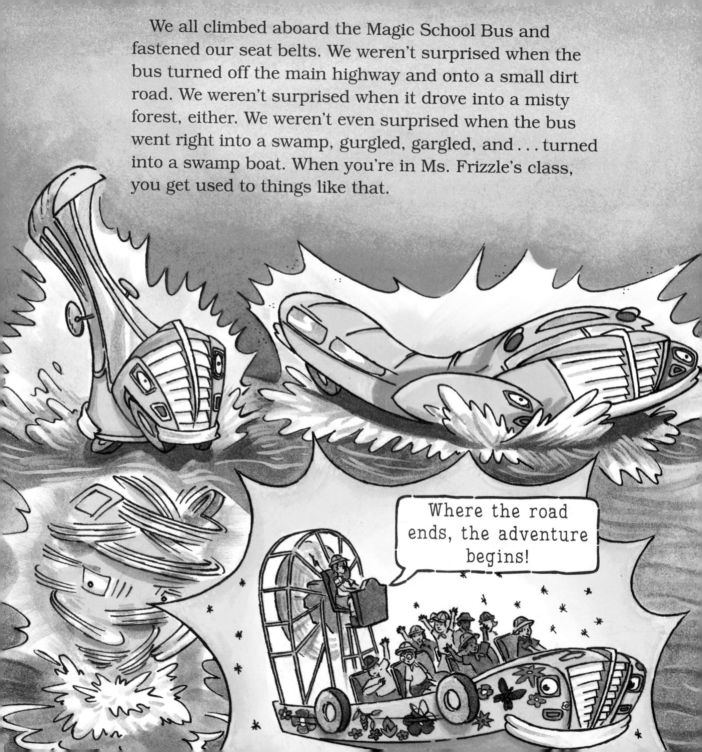

Where the road ends, the adventure begins!

The bus skimmed across the top of the swamp water. All around us we saw trees and flowers.

"What is this place, Ms. Frizzle?" asked Dorothy Ann.

"It's called Butterfly Bog," replied Ms. Frizzle.

Just then a swarm of beautiful yellow butterflies took off from a branch. A blue jay flew down and snatched one of the butterflies in its beak.

"Some mascot," said Janet. "If a blue jay can do that, what will the Bulldogs do to your soccer team?" The Bulldogs were the team we were supposed to play.

The bus stopped at a small, moss-covered island. "Here we are," announced Ms. Frizzle. "Bog Beast Landing."

This was getting *really* exciting! Soon we'd probably see a real, live Bog Beast! Carlos covered the bus with moss so it blended in with the surroundings. That way, the Bog Beast wouldn't be afraid to come close to us. We stayed very still and waited.

"According to my research, the best way to catch something is to use some kind of bait," whispered Dorothy Ann.

And Janet knew exactly what kind of bait was best. She smiled and picked up her butterfly net. "Like the biggest, juiciest butterfly in the bog," she said. She jumped off the bus and onto the island.

Janet's idea to catch a butterfly really upset Phoebe. "Janet, why don't you pick on someone your own size?" she shouted after her.

Ms. Frizzle thought *that* was a great idea. She reached under the dashboard and pulled out her portashrinker machine. She aimed the machine at Janet and Liz and pushed the button. She was going to shrink them! A light flashed. A loud bell rang.

Unfortunately, the portashrinker rays bounced right off the shiny metal charm that Liz wore around her neck. The rays came right back toward the bus! The next thing we knew, we — not Janet and Liz — were two inches high! Worst of all, the portashrinker had landed in the water. It was too wet to work!

That's when we heard Ms. Frizzle say something we thought we'd never hear. "Whoops," she said. "This wasn't supposed to happen."

"I don't care how small I am," declared Phoebe. "I've got butterflies to save!" She raced off to make sure the butterflies stayed away from Janet and Liz.

Then we heard a scream. We ran to Phoebe's rescue.

She was staring eye-to-eye with a long, snakelike monster. The monster seemed to be licking its chops. It looked hungry.

I think this is going to be one of those *memorable* field trips!

Bog Beast!

Even Ralphie was scared. "Okay, we've seen a Bog Beast," he said. "Now let's get out of here."

Ralphie tried to run off, but Ms. Frizzle pulled him back. "Not so fast, Ralphie," she said calmly. "Since you've never *seen* a Bog Beast, how can you be sure this *is* a Bog Beast?"

"It looks more like a snake to me," said Wanda.

"Except it doesn't *move* like a snake," Phoebe pointed out. "It *moves* like a caterpillar."

"Hey, it *is* a caterpillar," agreed Tim.

"A caterpillar pretending to be a snake," Carlos added.

Just then, a large green praying mantis landed in front of the caterpillar. It stood on its hind legs, blocking the caterpillar's path. The praying mantis was looking for lunch.

"Won't a praying mantis eat a caterpillar?" Dorothy Ann asked Tim.

The caterpillar reared up, wagged its head, and flicked something that looked like a tongue. The praying mantis hopped away quickly.

"Not if the praying mantis thinks the caterpillar is a snake," answered Tim.

"I get it!" Carlos shouted. "That caterpillar tricked its enemy by pretending to be something it isn't!"

Then Wanda remembered we were still looking for a name for our soccer team. "What if we call our team the Walker Elementary Caterpillars?"

"We'll get laughed out of the game!" answered Ralphie. "Besides, if we don't get back soon, there won't *be* any game!"

But that wasn't our only problem. We still had to stop Janet from catching the butterflies. There was no way we were going to let her feed them to the Bog Beast.

"It's just not fair, Ms. Frizzle," sobbed Phoebe as we watched Janet swing her net at a black-and-orange butterfly.

"I know." Ms. Frizzle smiled. "Janet doesn't stand a chance."

What did the Friz mean by that?

Janet lifted her net and grinned. "This one's a real juicy one," she told Liz. But just as Janet tried to capture the butterfly, it seemed to disappear.

"Okay, wiseguy, where are you?" Janet called out.

The butterfly's colored markings blended in with the log. Janet couldn't find it!

"I always say, if they can't see you, they can't eat you!" Ms. Frizzle laughed. Then she put two fingers in her mouth and whistled loudly. The bus pulled up. We all piled in.

Phoebe was still watching Janet. "Oh, no!" cried Phoebe. "Janet is going to catch that butterfly."

"You're mine, wimp!" Janet called to the butterfly. She lifted her net up in the air, and Liz fell off Janet's shoulder. *Splash!* Liz landed in the mud. In all the confusion, the butterfly flew away.

A big wave of brown mud washed over us. "Swamp swill!" yelled Carlos.

Arnold had had enough. "That's it!" he said. "I'm unshrinking us before Jumbo Janet crushes us all." Arnold took Ms. Frizzle's portashrinker and pushed the button. Nothing happened.

Then we heard a bell ring.

"What's that?" Arnold asked. He sounded a little nervous.

"The dew-dinger," explained Ms. Frizzle. "It dings when the portashrinker is too wet to work."

Ms. Frizzle handed a blow-dryer to Arnold. "Start drying," she said. Just then, we heard a loud scream.

"That's Janet!" Arnold told us. "I'd know that scream anywhere."

We tried to run and help her. But we were stopped in our tracks by a huge flash of black-and-yellow stripes! We were so surprised, we completely forgot about Janet.

Seems like the perfect mascot to me!

"Bog Beast!" Ralphie yelled.

Dorothy Ann looked at the black-and-yellow stripes. Then she looked at the butterfly and moth book. "It's not a Bog Beast," she said. "It's a zebra butterfly."

Ralphie blushed. "Well, it, uh . . . it just startled me with all its colors, that's all."

"See? Even though butterflies are small and pretty, they're *not* wimps!" Phoebe told Ralphie. "They trick you. They hide from you. They even scare you! That's how they stay alive!"

Now everyone wanted our team to be the Walker Elementary Butterflies. Except Ralphie. "Never!" he cried. "I'll play for the other team before anyone calls me a butterfly." And with that he walked away.

Before long, we heard Ralphie yell. We found him hiding behind the root of a mangrove tree. "It's a . . . it's a . . ."

Wanda laughed at Ralphie. "Yeah, we know. It's a Bog Beast."

Wanda looked up. Two huge black eyes stared back down at her. All of a sudden, Wanda wasn't laughing anymore. Nobody was!

"Bog Beast!" we all cried out at once.

But it wasn't a Bog Beast at all. It was a buckeye butterfly.
"Those eyes aren't real," Phoebe pointed out. "They just look like eyes to fool the enemy."

Butterflies were pretty tricky, *and* surprising — just the things we wanted our soccer team to be!

My, what big eyespots you have!

All the better to fool you with, my dear!

"Okay, Phoebe, you win," Ralphie said. "We'll be the Walker Elementary Butterflies!"

Phoebe led us all in a cheer. "Let's take our team to the skies!" she shouted.

"Let's be Walker Elementary Butterflies," we cheered back.

A big smile flashed across Ms. Frizzle's face. "If you insist," she said.

We heard a loud whirring sound. The next thing we knew, we were flying around in the Magic School Busserfly!

This isn't exactly what we meant.

The Magic School Busserfly spread its wings and took off. It made a low humming sound as it flew.

"So what do you think, class?" Ms. Frizzle asked us as we came in for a landing.

"It's certainly a new sensation," answered Dorothy Ann.

Just then, a giant face appeared in front of us. And it didn't seem friendly!

Well, as I always say,
when a butterfly — do
as the butterflies do.

I don't like
the sound of that.

Janet thought *we* were a butterfly — a *big, juicy* butterfly! She wanted to catch us.

"Janet's gonna feed us to the Bog Beast!" screamed Ralphie.

The Busserfly flew away from Janet. But Janet was a lot bigger than we were.

"She's gaining on us!" cried Keesha.

"Ms. Frizzle, what should we do?" Wanda asked.

Phoebe had an idea. "Is there a button that'll make us blend into our surroundings like real butterflies do?" she asked, pointing to the dashboard.

Ms. Frizzle nodded. "You might check for the camouflage box — if you can find it."

Phoebe reached under the dashboard and opened the camouflage box. There were a lot of buttons. Phoebe couldn't be sure which one would make us blend in with the scenery.

"Oh, no! Which one is it?" she asked.

Suddenly Janet's net came down on top of us. "Come on, Phoebe, you're our last hope!" cried Ralphie.

Phoebe wasn't about to give up. "Think butterfly . . ." she mumbled to herself. "That's it! I'll surprise her with colors!" She flipped the color switches on the camouflage box. The bus turned red, yellow, orange, and blue!

"And now to trick her with eyespots!" Phoebe exclaimed. With a flick of a switch the bus grew huge, bulging eyespots.

Janet reached under the net and grabbed for us. But the bus opened its wings really wide!

Janet took one look at the bus's bright colors and bulging eyespots and screamed! She thought the bus was a Bog Beast. Janet jumped back, lifting the net with her. We were free!

"What a field trip," said Arnold as he bounced down into his seat. He landed right on top of the portashrinker. Presto! The Magic School Bus changed back to its real size.

Janet spotted the bus and ran to us. "I saw the Bog Beast!" she shouted.

"Did it look anything like this butterfly?" Tim asked. He showed her a picture that he had drawn of our bus as a butterfly.

Boy, was Janet shocked to find out that *we* were the Bog Beast. Ms. Frizzle explained that a Bog Beast can be whatever you want it to be. In this case, it happened to be a Bog Beast Butterfly!

The Bulldogs couldn't believe it when they saw our mascot. But they were even *more* surprised when the Bog Beast Butterflies won the soccer game! Phoebe had been right all along. Butterflies weren't just small and beautiful. They were full of surprises!

As I always say, there's no surprise like butterflies!

Dear Editor,
at the Great Moth Majority
e steamed. We know that there
e eight times as many moths
s there are butterflies in this
world. Scientists are still
inding new ones! But you don't
mention these winged wonders —
not even once! We demand equal
time for our favorite flying
friends, the moths.

Signed,
The Members of the Great Moth
Majority Fan Club

Dear Editor,
After reading your book, I got the eyedea
that you didn't know the eyespots on
moths and butterflies do a lot more than
surprise teeny tiny kids in teeny tiny
buses — or the cousins of teeny tiny kids
in teeny tiny buses. So I wanted to tell
you that when a bird tries to catch a
moth or a butterfly it goes for the eyes.
And if it goes for the eyespots, all it gets
is a beak full of wing.

Yours truly,
Eyedeal Information

Dear Editor,
It was terrible to see Janet running
around with a net trying to catch
butterflies. Moths and butterflies
should be left alone. Maybe
next time you should stick
Janet in a big net!

Sincerely,
A Friend to Nature

A Note to Teachers, Parents, and Kids

The beauty, color, and variety of butterflies and moths have always fascinated people. But, as you can imagine, life is not easy for these "flying flowers." Butterflies and moths seem so fragile — especially against their enemies, many of whom are larger and stronger than they are.

But **appearances can be deceiving!** Just like other insects and animals, butterflies and moths have many deceptive and unique ways to keep from being eaten. Many butterflies and moths use camouflage techniques to hide from their predators. Some, like the caterpillars of the long-tailed skipper, simply hide out in rolled-up shelters made of leaves. Others, especially those with muted browns and greens in their wings, use their coloring to blend in with the surroundings. It also helps that butterflies and moths have an uncanny ability to stay very, very still. Their behavior and coloring work well together to convince predators that they're not really there!

What about those butterflies and moths with bright coloring? They can't blend in. So they try to trick their predators into going away. That's when eyespots come in handy. They can make a moth, butterfly, or caterpillar seem much bigger — and more dangerous — than it really is. And that's often enough to scare off an unsuspecting bird, mammal, or snake!

Ms. Frizzle